Little Red Riding Hood

Retold by Alan Trussell-Cullen

Illustrated by Steven Pileggi

HAMERAY
PUBLISHING GROUP

Once there was a little girl who lived by a forest.
She always wore a red coat with a hood.
Her grandma had made it for her.
Everyone called her Little Red Riding Hood.

One day her mom asked her to take some cookies to Grandma.
Grandma was sick.
Grandma's house was deep in the forest.
"Don't talk to anyone on the way," said her mom.
"The forest is not safe."

Little Red Riding Hood skipped along the path to Grandma's house.
Along the way she met a woodcutter.
He was chopping down a tree.
"Hi there, Little Red Riding Hood.
Where are you going?" he asked.

"I'm taking these cookies to my grandma,"
said Little Red Riding Hood.
"But my mom said not to talk to anyone,
so I'd better say goodbye."
"Your mom is right.
The forest is not safe. Goodbye," said the woodcutter.

A little further on, she met a wolf.
"Hi there, Little Red Riding Hood! Where are you going?" said the wolf.
"I'm taking these cookies to my grandma," said Little Red Riding Hood.
"But my mom said not to talk to anyone, so I'd better say goodbye."

Little Red Riding Hood skipped along the path again.
"I know a shortcut to Grandma's house,"
said the wolf with a nasty smile.
He ran off through the trees.

When he got to Grandma's house, he knocked on the door.
"Who is it?" said Grandma.
"It's me, Little Red Riding Hood," said the Wolf.
"Come in, dear," said Grandma.

But when Grandma saw the wolf, she was scared.
She jumped out of bed and ran down to the basement to hide.
The nasty wolf locked the door to the basement.

Just then Little Red Riding Hood knocked on the door.
The wolf pulled on Grandma's nightgown and jumped into her bed.
"Who is it?" said the wolf.
He tried to sound like Grandma.

"It's me," said Little Red Riding Hood.
"Come in, dear. I'm in bed," said the wolf.

"Oh Grandma, what big eyes you have!" said Little Red Riding Hood.
"All the better to see you with, my dear," said the wolf.
"But Grandma, what big ears you have!" said Little Red Riding Hood.
"All the better to hear you with, my dear," said the wolf.

"But Grandma, what big teeth you have!" said Little Red Riding Hood.

"All the better to eat you with!" said the wolf, as he jumped
out of bed.

But just at that moment the woodcutter burst into the house.
He chased the wolf away with his axe.
Grandma began to bang on the basement door.
"Oh Grandma!" said Little Red Riding Hood as she let her out.
"Thank goodness you are safe!"

Then they all sat down to a cup of tea.
"These cookies are so good!" said Grandma.
"I am feeling much better now.
Thank you, Little Red Riding Hood!"